A NOTE TO PARENTS

When your children are ready to "step into reading," giving them the right books is as crucial to their development as giving them the right food to eat. **Step into Reading®** books feature exciting stories and information reinforced with lively, colorful illustrations that make learning to read fun, satisfying, and rewarding. We have even taken *extra* steps to keep your child engaged by offering Step into Reading Sticker books, Step into Reading Math books, and Step into Reading Phonics books, in addition to fabulous fiction and nonfiction.

Learning to read, Step by Step:

- **Super Early** books (Preschool–Kindergarten) support pre-reading skills. Parent and child can engage in "see and say" reading using the strong picture cues and the few simple words on each page.
- **Early** books (Preschool–Kindergarten) let emergent readers tackle one or two short sentences of large type per page.
- **Step 1** books (Preschool–Grade 1) have the same easy-to-read type as Early, but with more words per page.
- **Step 2** books (Grades 1–3) offer longer and slightly more difficult text while introducing contractions and clauses. Children are often drawn to our exciting natural science nonfiction titles at this level.
- **Step 3** books (Grades 2–3) present paragraphs, chapters, and fully developed plot lines in fiction and nonfiction.
- **Step 4** books (Grades 2–4) feature thrilling nonfiction illustrated with exciting photographs for independent as well as reluctant readers.

Remember: The grade levels assigned to the six steps are intended only as guides. Some children move through all six steps rapidly; others climb the steps over a period of a few years. Either way, these books will help children "step into reading" for life!

www.randomhouse.com/kids/disney

Library of Congress Cataloging-in-Publication Data
Shealy, Dennis R.
Pirates attack! / by Dennis Shealy.
    p. cm.— (Step into reading) "A Step 3 Book."
SUMMARY: In a space version of the classic Treasure Island, the boy Jim and the
cyborg cook, John Silver, travel the galaxy in search of Captain Flint's treasure.
ISBN 0-7364-2021-5 — ISBN 0-7364-8014-5 (alk. paper)
[1. Pirates—Fiction. 2. Buried treasure—Fiction. 3.
Friendship—Fiction. 4. Science fiction.] I. Title. II. Series.
PZ7.S53767 Pi 2002   [Fic]—dc21   2002008730

Step into Reading®

Disney's TREASURE PLANET

Pirates Attack!

A Step 3 Book

Adapted by Dennis Shealy
Illustrated by the Disney Storyboard Artists

Random House 🏠 New York

Pirates . . .

They were enemies of all honest spacers. The most feared of all pirates was Captain Nathaniel Flint.

Flint and his gang would mysteriously swoop in from nowhere and attack. Then, gathering the riches, the pirates would vanish without a trace. For hundreds of years, stories passed from spacer to spacer about Flint's treasure. It was hidden somewhere in the galaxy—the loot of a thousand worlds!

There was one man who wanted that treasure more than anyone else. But his dream came at a heavy price. In his search for the treasure, an accident had almost cost him his life. He was now half man and half machine: a cyborg! Still, he would not give up. The treasure was going to be his. . . .

Chapter 1: Beware the Cyborg

A large shadow loomed in the *Legacy*'s dark galley. Small motors whirred and clicked as the hulking figure stepped into the light. Jim Hawkins, the new cabin boy, gasped. The ship's cook was a cyborg!

Mr. Arrow, the *Legacy*'s first officer, introduced Jim to John Silver.

"Jimbo!" said Silver, holding out his metal hand. Jim frowned.

Silver knew that Jim was an important link to the treasure. But he also knew that the boy could get in his way. Jim had joined the *Legacy*'s crew because he had the map to Treasure Planet. The boy had been given the map by a stranger, Billy Bones. With his dying breath, Bones had handed Jim the map and warned him, "Beware the cyborg!"

The cyborg shoved a bowl of steaming bonzabeast stew into Jim's hands. Jim was about to taste it when his spoon turned into a bubbly pink blob! Then it turned into a straw and sucked up all the stew.

"Morph, you jiggle-headed blob o' mischief! So that's where you was hidin'!" Silver chuckled.

"He's a morph," he told Jim. "I rescued the little shape shifter on Proteus One. We've been together ever since."

Morph chirped and changed shape. Jim laughed at the lovable creature, but he was wary of the cyborg. Silver noticed.

"These gears were tough to get used to, but they do come in handy," Silver said cheerily as he chopped and diced some vegetables with his mechanical hand.

Suddenly, the ship's whistle blew.

"Off with ya, lad, and watch the launch!" Silver said. He knew Jim wanted

to see the *Legacy* cast off. Silver was eager to make Jim like him.

But as the boy left, a scowl crossed Silver's face. "We'd best be keepin' an eye on that one," he said to Morph.

Chapter 2: Loose Ends

The commander of the *Legacy,* Captain
Amelia, had assigned Jim to be Silver's
cabin boy. She hoped Jim could learn a
lesson or two during the voyage.

Over time, Silver taught Jim more than
just how to scrub the deck. He showed him
how to be a fine spacer. Silver even began

to care about the lad. But he still wanted
the map.

One day, as Jim and Silver sat talking
below deck, Silver's mechanical leg stiffened
up. Morph happily turned into a wrench
and Silver began to adjust his gears.

Jim had been curious about Silver's
mechanical arm and leg since he had first
laid eyes on them.

"How'd that happen, anyway?"
he asked.

"You give up a few things chasin' a
dream," Silver sighed.

Suddenly, the ship lurched! It was being drawn into a black hole!

The crew tried to control the ship, while Jim tied off all their lifelines as Silver had taught him. "All lines secured, Captain!" he yelled—and just in the nick of time! The black hole's gravity was beginning to pull the crew right off the deck.

Dr. Doppler, the scientist, helped Captain Amelia navigate. Soon, Amelia had safely steered the ship across the waves of crackling energy. The crew cheered as the *Legacy* escaped the pull of the black hole.

But when Captain Amelia called for her first mate, Mr. Arrow, there was no answer. In all the chaos, he'd been lost!

Everyone turned to look at Jim. They thought it was *his* fault Mr. Arrow had been sucked into space! After all, Jim was in charge of the lifelines.

Silver felt sorry for the boy. Then he noticed the spider-like crew member Scroop fiddling with the end of Arrow's rope. So it wasn't Jim's fault after all! Scroop had cut the first mate's lifeline.

"You listen to me, Jim Hawkins," Silver said later when he found the boy alone. "You got the makin's of greatness in ya. But you got to take the helm and chart your own course." As Jim leaned over to hug Silver, the cyborg gave in and comforted Jim. Silver was a pirate, but he also had a heart—he had grown fond of the boy.

Chapter 3: Mutiny!

The next morning, Morph playfully jumped into Jim's boot and hopped away. The boy chased the blob into the galley. Jim tumbled into a barrel just as he grabbed Morph. From inside, he heard Silver's crew enter. The pirates thought they were alone.

"Disobey my orders again like that stunt you pulled with Mr. Arrow," Silver growled at Scroop, "and so help me you'll be joinin' him!"

"Methinks you have a *soft* spot for the boy," Scroop hissed.

Silver couldn't let the crew know how he felt about Jim. "I only care about one thing . . . Flint's treasure," Silver replied. "You think I would risk it all for the sake of some little whelp?"

Jim was devastated. He had grown to trust Silver.

"Planet ho!" the lookout yelled from his perch in the crow's nest. The *Legacy* had finally reached Treasure Planet!

The pirates scrambled up the stairs. But soon Silver returned below deck to get his spyglass and found Jim there. The old pirate realized that Jim must have overheard the whole conversation!

Silver hesitated. Though he was fond of the boy, he knew he had to catch Jim. Otherwise the lad could warn Captain Amelia—and Silver would never get his precious treasure.

"We move now!" Silver roared. The pirates cheered and raised the flag. The mutiny had begun!

At that moment, Jim was telling Doppler and Amelia about the trouble ahead. The three quickly raced to the longboats with the map . . . with the pirates in close pursuit!

Morph mistook all the excitement
for a game. He snatched the globe-like map
from Jim's pocket. Jim chased after him.
Then Silver appeared. He would get the
map, by thunder, no matter what he had
to do! Silver and Jim both tried to coax
the map away from the confused little blob.
But Jim grabbed it first! Then he leaped
onto the longboat where Amelia and
Doppler were waiting. The longboat
launched from the ship at full speed.

"Hold your fire!" Silver yelled at his crew. "Or we'll lose the map!"

Despite Silver's order, one of the pirates fired a laser cannon and hit the longboat, causing it to crash-land on Treasure Planet. Silver quickly ordered his crew to follow Jim and retrieve the map once and for all.

Chapter 4: Treasure Planet

On the surface of Treasure Planet, Jim and
his friends met a strange robot named
B.E.N. The robot had once worked for
Captain Flint, but he couldn't remember
where the treasure was hidden. Flint had
removed B.E.N.'s memory circuit. But B.E.N.
did have a home, and it was the perfect
place to hide from the pirates.

Silver and his crew quickly discovered
the hideout. He waved a white flag in hopes
of negotiating with Jim.

"Whatever you heard back there," Silver said, "I didn't mean a word of it. We can both walk away rich as kings."

"I'm gonna make sure you don't see one drubloon of *my* treasure!" Jim snarled.

Silver was enraged. "Either I get that map by dawn tomorrow, or I'LL BLAST YA ALL TO KINGDOM COME!" he shouted.

The pirate would have been even angrier had he known the truth. Jim didn't really have the map—it was still aboard the *Legacy*!

Silver and the pirates went to sleep. Little did they know that Jim had snuck into their camp and stolen the longboats. When Silver awoke he realized what Jim had done. He became suspicious—maybe Jim did not

have the map. Why else would he risk such a dangerous move?

But with Jim gone, Silver figured it would be easier to get inside B.E.N.'s house and wait for his return.

That's just fine, Jimbo, Silver thought. *While you're up there, I'll be down here plannin' me own surprise.*

Chapter 5: The Map

Not long afterward, Jim returned with the map and crept back into B.E.N.'s house. Silver quickly sprang his trap. He had Amelia and Doppler held hostage. The pirates leaped up and grabbed the map! But Silver could not open it. He shoved the map into Jim's hand and ordered the boy to unlock it.

"You want the map? Then you're taking me, too!" cried Jim.

Silver smiled wickedly and said, "We'll take 'em all."

Jim unlocked the map. The mechanical orb slowly began to open. With a burst of light, the map projected a swirling green trail. Using the trail as a guide, Jim led the whole group through the forest.

"We're getting close, lads. I can smell it!" Silver said as the map's path continued toward some thick plants. His lifelong dream was finally about to come true!

The pirates quickly cleared the path . . . but the only thing that was waiting for them was the edge of a cliff—and a three-thousand-foot drop!

Silver started to get angry.

He thought Jim was trying to trick him—until the boy discovered some ancient symbols on the ground at the edge of the cliff. The symbols matched the ones on the map. Jim placed the spherical map on top of the pattern. Suddenly a huge triangle of light appeared!

Finally, Flint's secret had been uncovered—it was a portal, or gateway, to anywhere in the universe!

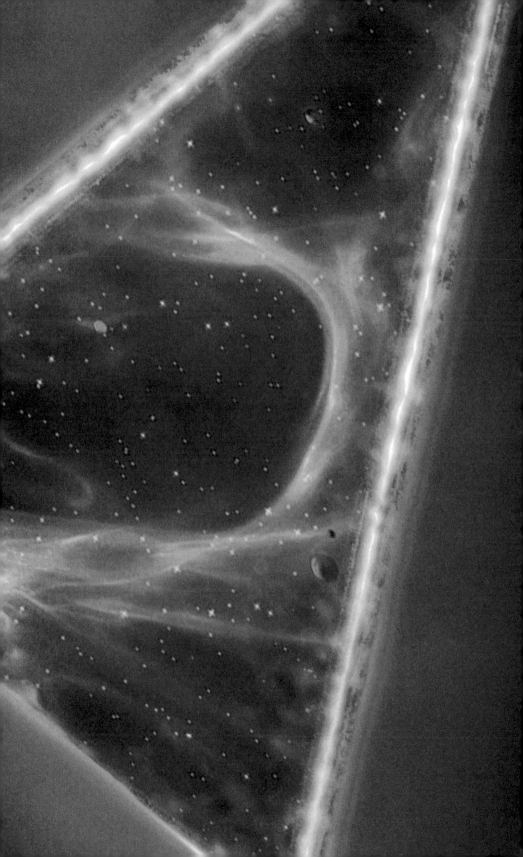

Nearby, Jim found a control panel.
He looked at it closely and realized it was
a map of the universe.

He touched the center of Treasure Planet on the panel, and the portal opened.

Jim walked into the portal and disappeared. Silver took a deep breath and followed. At long last, Silver found himself standing before unimaginable riches—the loot of a thousand worlds!

Chapter 6: The Loot of a Thousand Worlds

The heaps of gold and precious metals from around the universe glowed. Gems and crystals sparkled like stars. Flint's ancient pirate ship rested nearby.

"A lifetime of searching," Silver said in awe as he lifted dozens of gold coins and jewels, "and I can finally touch it!"

But Silver and the pirates were so busy marveling at the riches that they didn't notice Jim leading B.E.N. toward Flint's ship.

On the ship, Flint's skeleton still sat on his pirate's throne. Jim noticed an old computer chip in Flint's bony fingers. It looked as if it just might fit into the slot in the back of B.E.N.'s head. Jim tried it. Suddenly, the crazy robot began to regain his memory.

Then B.E.N. started to remember everything—including something about Flint's treasure. Something important. Suddenly, he shouted, "Booby trap!"

Flint had set a trap years before to protect his treasure. Now, explosions rocked the massive cavern as deadly energy beams came to life! The pirates tried desperately to flee back through the portal. But Silver, who had searched so long for the treasure, stayed behind.

Silver saw Jim at the helm of Flint's ship, trying to start its ancient engine. The cyborg dashed aboard.

"I've come too far to let you stand between me and the treasure," Silver said. Jim grabbed a sword and growled, "Get *back*!"

Suddenly, the rising ship was hit by an energy beam as the core of Treasure Planet broke apart. The ship lurched forward—and Jim fell overboard!

Holding on to the ship as it drifted away, Silver tried to reach Jim, who was barely clinging to a ledge.

Silver knew he couldn't save Jim *and* the treasure! There was only one choice for the pirate to make.

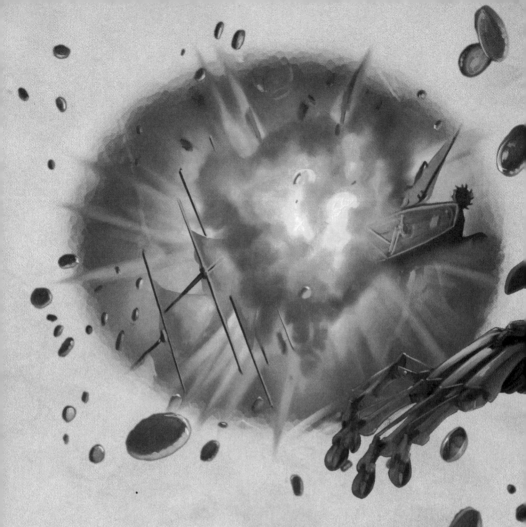

Silver let go of the last remaining treasure and reached for Jim.

Just as he grabbed the boy, an energy beam vaporized Flint's ship and all his loot. Silver protected the lad.

Now there was no time to waste. Silver and Jim raced back through the portal!

Chapter 7: The Ol' Scalawag

On the other side of the portal, the *Legacy* swooped down with Doppler at the helm and B.E.N. navigating. But Treasure Planet was about to explode! They didn't have enough time to get away!

Suddenly, Jim had an idea. If the map's portal could open to anywhere in the universe, maybe they could use it to escape. He quickly grabbed spare parts from the ship's cannon and started to construct a solar surfer.

He was going to fly back and open the portal for the *Legacy* to pass through.

Silver quickly began to help his young friend. "What do ya need, Jim?" he asked gently. Then he used his cyborg arm to help Jim weld an engine to a metal plate.

When they were done, Jim leaped from the *Legacy* and shot toward the portal on his solar surfer. Silver watched the lad . . . and wished him luck. Luckily, the portal controls were still intact. Jim reached for the symbol for the spaceport Crescentia just before the whole planet exploded!

"Jimbo! Ya done it, lad!" Silver proudly cheered as the ship was transported millions of miles from the shattered Treasure Planet to Crescentia.

Doppler, Amelia, B.E.N., and Morph ran over to hug Jim. They were happy to be alive—treasure or no treasure!

While they celebrated, the old cyborg tried to slip away unnoticed, knowing that Captain Amelia would soon put him in jail if he stayed.

Jim's shadow fell over Silver and Morph as they prepared to leave.

"What say you ship out with us, lad?" Silver suggested—but he already knew Jim's answer.

The two friends hugged, knowing they would not see each other again.

"Morphy, I've got a little job for ya," said Silver.

"I need ya ta keep an eye on this here pup. Will ya do me that favor?"

Morph nodded happily, fondly nuzzling Silver goodbye.

Wiping the tears from his eye, Silver pushed off, leaving Jim and Morph behind.

"Stay out of trouble, you ol' scalawag," Jim called out.

"Why, Jimbo, when have I ever done otherwise?" Silver replied with a sly grin.

The old pirate chuckled, and Jim could hear his laughter long after the skiff had faded from view.

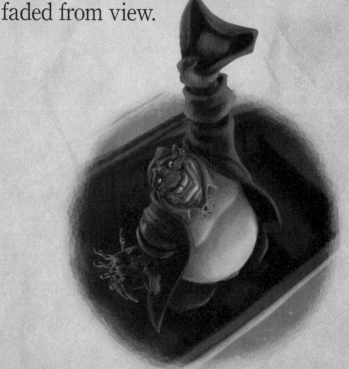